DOWN BY THE COOL of THE POOL

Tony Mitton illustrated by Guy Parker-Rees

ORCHARD BOOKS

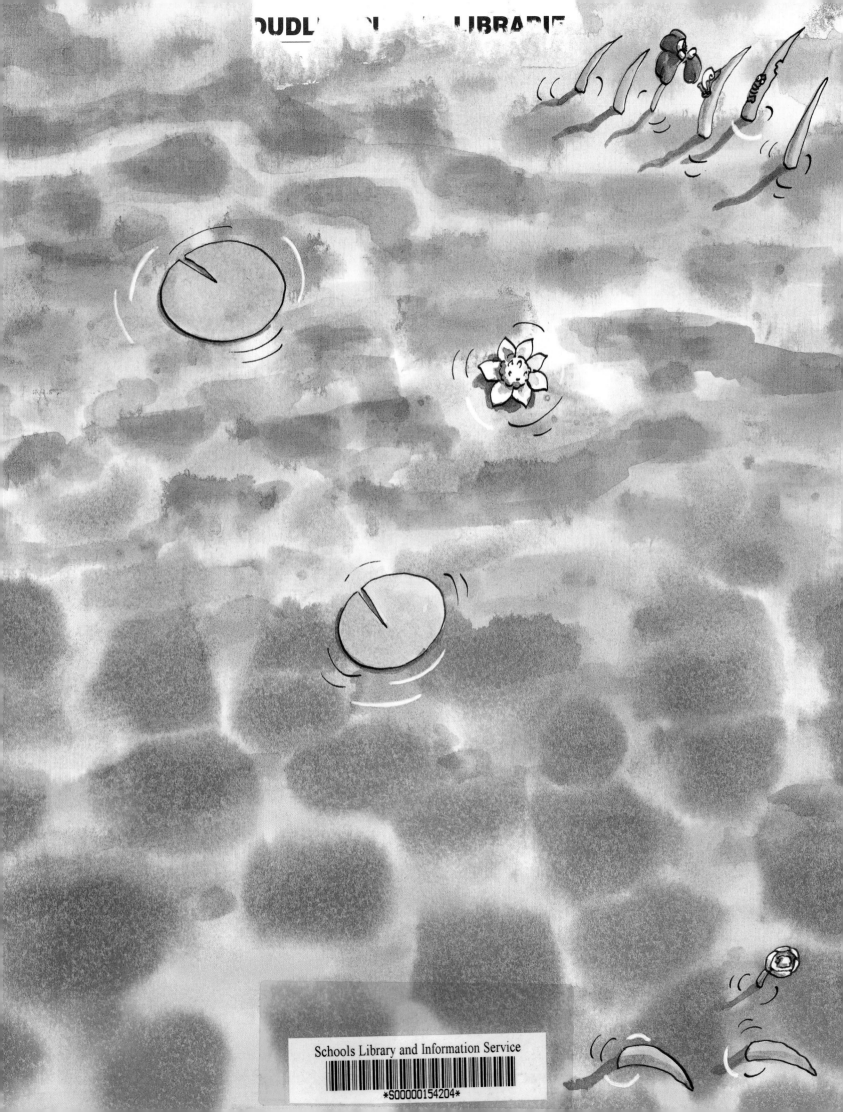

For George, Harriet, Doris and Guthrie,
and the cool of the pool in France – T.M.

For the lovely chucklesome little Joe – G.P-R.

ORCHARD BOOKS
96 Leonard Street, London EC2A 4XD
Orchard Books Australia
Unit 31/56 O'Riordan Street, Alexandria, NSW 2015
1 84121 853 7
First published in Great Britain in 2001
Text © Tony Mitton 2001
Illustrations © Guy Parker-Rees 2001
The right of Tony Mitton to be identified as the author and
Guy Parker-Rees to be identified as the illustrator
of this work has been asserted by them in accordance
with the Copyright, Designs and Patents Act 1988.
A CIP catalogue record for this book is available from the British Library.
2 4 6 8 10 9 7 5 3 1
Printed in Hong Kong/China

Duck came to see.
"I can dance too.
But not like you.
I can flap."

So Duck went "flap"

and Frog cried,

"**Wheeeee!**

Can you dance like me?"

Down by the cool of the pool.

Sheep came to see.
"I can dance too.
But not like you.
I can stamp."

So Sheep went

stamp,

Pig went "wiggle",

Duck went "flap",

and Frog cried "Wheeeee!"

Can you dance like me?"

Down by the cool of the pool.

Goat butted in with a **skip** and a **hop**,

and Frog cried, **"Wheeeee!** That's great! Don't stop."

Then Playful Pony began to **prance**

and Donkey **drummed** his hoofbeat dance,

With a **stamp**, and a **"wiggle"**,

But did that stop them?

We're having fun, dancing our dance **in** the cool of the pool!"

And they **splished** and **splashed** till their dance was done,

then away they drifted

and down went the sun,

PLOP!

even Frog... was gone.